KT-160-541

**T**his is George.

He was a good little monkey and always very curious.

Today George and his friend the man with the yellow hat joined

Mrs Gray and her class on their field trip to the fire station.

The Fire Chief was waiting for them right next to a big red fire engine.

"Welcome!" he said, and he led everyone upstairs to begin their tour.

# MARGRET & H.A. REY's

## *Curious George*

## and the Fire-fighters

WALKER BOOKS
AND SUBSIDIARIES
LONDON • BOSTON • SYDNEY • AUCKLAND

First published in Great Britain 2006
by Walker Books Ltd, 87 Vauxhall Walk, London SE11 5HJ

8 10 9 7

© 2004 Houghton Mifflin Company
Curious George® is a registered trademark of Houghton Mifflin Company
Published by arrangement with Houghton Mifflin Company

This book has been typeset in Gill Sans MT Schoolbook
Illustrated in the style of H. A. Rey by Anna Grossnickle Hines

Printed in China

All rights reserved. No part of this book may be reproduced, transmitted or
stored in an information retrieval system in any form or by any means, graphic,
electronic or mechanical, including photocopying, taping and recording,
without prior written permission from the publisher.

British Library Cataloguing in Publication Data:
a catalogue record for this book is available from the British Library

ISBN 978-0-7445-7049-6

www.walker.co.uk

There was a kitchen with a big table, and there were snacks for everyone. The Fire Chief told them all about being a fire-fighter. George tried hard to pay attention, but there were so many things for a little monkey to explore. Like that shiny brass pole in the corner...

Where did that pole go? George was curious.

Why, it went back downstairs! There was the great big fire engine. There was a map of the city. And there was a whole wall full of coats and hats and big black boots!

George had an idea.
First he stepped into
a pair of boots.

Next, he picked out a helmet.

And, finally, George put on a jacket.
He was a fire-fighter!

Suddenly ... BRRRIINNGG!

The fire-fighters all rushed in.

"This is not my helmet!" said one.

"My boots are too big!" said another.

"Hurry! Hurry!" called the Fire Chief. A bright red light on the map of the city told him just where the fire was. There was no time to waste!

One by one, the fire-fighters jumped into the fire engine.

And so did George.

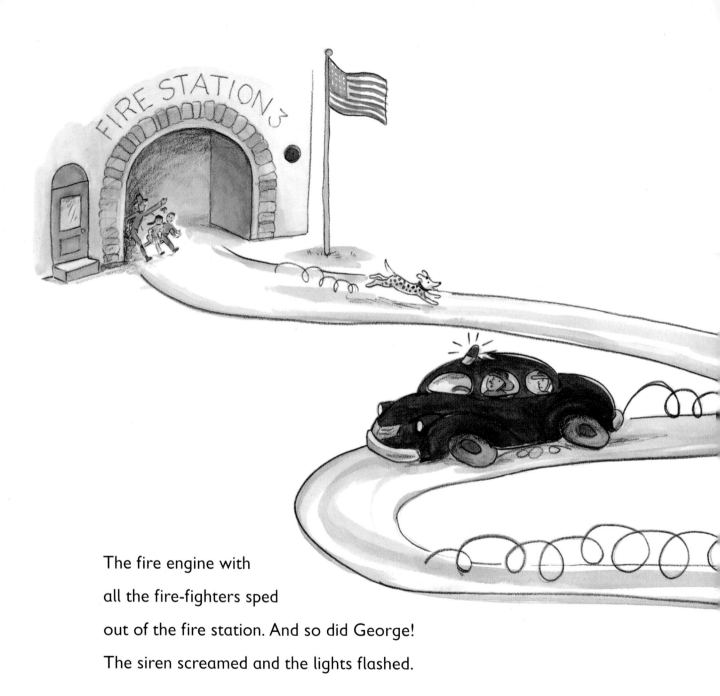

The fire engine with
all the fire-fighters sped
out of the fire station. And so did George!
The siren screamed and the lights flashed.

The engine turned right. Then it turned left.

"WHOO WHOO WHOO," went the horn

and George held on tight.

And just like that the fire engine and all the fire-fighters pulled up to a pizza parlour on Main Street. Smoke was coming out of a window in the back and a crowd was gathering in the street.

"Thank goodness you're here!" cried the cook.

The fire-fighters rushed off the truck and started
unwinding their hoses. They knew just what to do.
And George was ready to help.
He climbed up on the hose reel...

One of the fire-fighters saw George trying to help,

and he took George by the arm and led him out of the way.

"A fire is no place for a monkey!" he said to George.

"You stay here where it's safe." George felt terrible.

George sat on the bench and looked around. Next to him on the ground was a bucket full of balls. George reached in and took one out. It fitted in his hand just right, like the apple he'd had for a snack.

A little girl was watching George.

He tried to give her the ball,

but she was too frightened.

George took another ball.

And another.

"Look," a boy said.

"That monkey is juggling!"

The boy took a ball and tossed it to George, but it went too high.

George climbed up onto the fire engine to get it.

Now George had four balls to juggle. He threw the balls higher
and higher. He juggled with his hands. He juggled with his feet.
He could do all kinds of tricks!

The boy threw another ball to George. George threw a ball back to the boy. The little girl reached down and picked up a ball, too. Soon all the children were throwing and catching, back and forth.

19

The Fire Chief came to tell everyone that the fire was out. Just then, the little girl laughed and said, "Look, Mummy – a fire monkey!"

"Hey!" called the Fire Chief. "What are you doing up there?"

"What a wonderful idea," the little girl's mother said to the Fire Chief, "bringing this brave little monkey to help children when they're frightened."

"Oh," the Fire Chief said. "Well, er, thank you."

Before long the fire engine was back at the fire station, where
a familiar voice called, "George!" It was the man with the yellow hat.
"This little monkey had quite an adventure," said one of
the fire-fighters. "Is everyone all right?" asked Mrs Gray.

"Yes, it was just a small fire," said the Fire Chief. "And George was a big help." Now the field trip was coming to an end. But there was one more treat in store...

All the children got to take a ride around the neighbourhood on the
shiny red fire engine, and they each got their very own fire helmet.
Even George! And it was just the right size for a brave little monkey.